THE GIGGLING GHOST Girl Scout MYSTERY

First Edition ©2012 Carole Marsh/Gallopade International/Peachtree City, GA
Current Edition ©July 2015
Ebook edition ©2012
All rights reserved.
Manufactured in Peachtree City, GA

Carole Marsh Mysteries™ and its skull colophon are the property of Carole Marsh and
Gallopade International. Published by Gallopade International/Carole Marsh Books.
Printed in the United States of America.

This book is not authorized, approved, licensed, or endorsed by Girl Scouts of the USA.
The GIRL SCOUT name, mark, and all associated trademarks and logotypes are owned
by Girl Scouts of the USA.

Editor: Janice Baker
Assistant Editor: Sherri Smith Brown
Cover Design: Vicki DeJoy
Content Design: Randolyn Friedlander

Thank you to Sage Martin, Madeline Hervey, Avery Longmeyer, Ella Longmeyer (all real
Girl Scouts!) for agreeing to let us photograph them.

Gallopade is proud to be a member and supporter of these educational organizations
and associations:

American Booksellers Association
American Library Association
International Reading Association
National Association for Gifted Children
The National School Supply and Equipment Association
The National Council for the Social Studies
Museum Store Association
Association of Partners for Public Lands
Association of Booksellers for Children
Association for the Study of African American Life and History
National Alliance of Black School Educators

Dear Readers,

I'm so excited about *The Giggling Ghost Girl Scout Mystery!*

I have often had granddaughter Christina's troop camped out in wall-to-wall sleeping bags in the downstairs of my home in Savannah, just a few blocks from the Juliette Gordon Low Birthplace. They always have so much fun getting up early and gallivanting all around town to see the many beautiful squares in the Historic District, the fountain in Forsyth Park, eating ice cream at Leopold's, and many other fun "Girl Scout things!" Most of all—they like to giggle!

Many of the places you read about in this story are real—you can actually visit them, and use the Scavenger Hunt in the back of the book, if you wish—to "check-off" places as you see or visit them!

It's an exciting time in Girl Scouting—the 100th anniversary! But you know, to me, the really exciting time was way back when "Daisy" had her amazing brainstorm that produced the Girl Scouts! What a great gal! What a great idea!! Scouting is a wonderful opportunity for girls, and I am so proud that my daughter, and now granddaughters, have been troop leaders or members through the years.

And now, grab a box of your favorite cookies—Girl Scout cookies, of course—and join the girl characters in this book as they encounter history, mystery, legend, lore, and so much more...in search of the Giggling Ghost!

Giggling allowed!
Happy reading and happy Girl Scouting,

Carole Marsh
from my Writing Gazebo in
"The Most Haunted City in America"...
Savannah, Georgia

TABLE OF CONTENTS

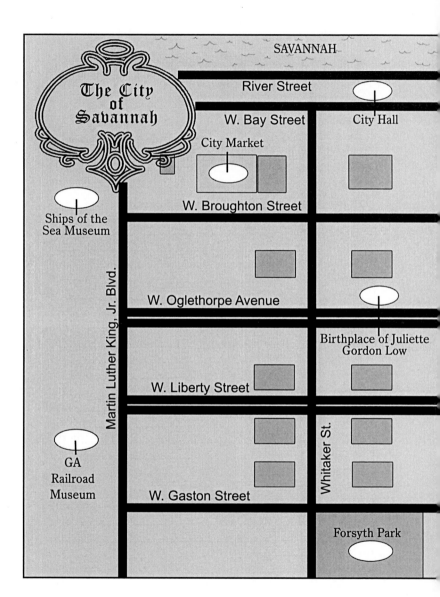

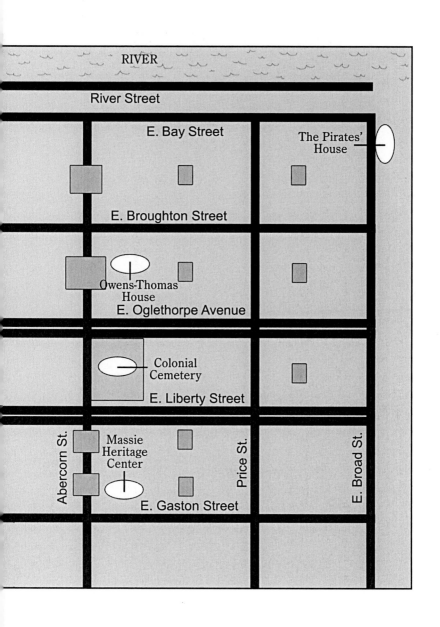

1

SAVANNAH BOUND!

BLAM!! SPLAT!! Grant burst into Christina's bedroom like a mini-tornado and nosedived straight onto her bed, scattering neatly piled clothes. He sprang up and started bouncing; his unruly blond hair swooshed up and down.

"I'm going on a shrimp boat! I'm going on a shrimp boat!" he sang.

THUMP! Christina's backpack fell off the bed. Her khaki Girl Scout sash, covered with brightly colored metal pins, slid to the floor.

"GRANT!" yelled Christina. "What are you doing?" Her stick-straight brown hair flipped into her eyes as she spun around to stare at him. "I'm packing for Savannah! Now you've messed up everything!"

Grant back-flipped from the bed into the middle of the room. His cousins, Ella and Avery, giggled uncontrollably. Christina's two friends, Grace and Amber, tried to hold back their laughter. Christina's brown eyes glared at her little brother.

Avery tugged Christina's arm. "Come on, Christina. I'll help you pick up things."

"Do a good turn daily!" said Ella, jumping up to help. "What's a shrimp boat, Grant?" she asked.

"Papa says it's a boat that goes out and catches shrimp!" replied Grant. "We're going to Tie-Bee Island." He looked puzzled. "I wonder how you tie a bee—do you use thread?"

Christina giggled. "You mean *Tybee Island*, Grant," she corrected. "It's an island just east of Savannah."

"That sounds like fun!" said Grace. She plucked Christina's sash from the floor. "Look at all these badges and pins you have!" Grace began to jive around the room. "I'm so happy to be going to Savannah!" she sang. "I can't wait for the Girl Scout Camporee! And we have three whole days to see Savannah before it even begins!"

12

The girls were headed to the National Girl Scout Camporee at Fort Stewart, just a few miles from Savannah. It was the 100th anniversary of the founding of the Girl Scouts, and the Camporee was going to be a spectacular event this year. Girls from all over the United States were coming to Savannah.

Christina, Grant, Ella, and Avery's grandparents, Mimi and Papa, had a home in the lovely old historic district of Savannah. Mimi had invited everyone to stay there for a few days. They could explore Savannah before the big event began later in the week.

"I love Savannah!" said Amber, her brown eyes twinkling. "I went there with my troop when I was younger. It was in the spring, and flowers were blooming everywhere. It was beautiful!"

Each of the girls was at a different level of scouting. Tiny, blond, blue-eyed Ella was a Daisy. Her cheerleader sister, Avery, was a Brownie. Grace was a Junior Girl Scout, and Amber was a Cadette. Christina, the oldest of the group, was a Senior Girl Scout.

"I have to finish my summer honors history project on General James Oglethorpe while we are there," Christina told the girls. "He was the founder of Savannah. I have a lot of research to do, but I can show you around the town. And you can do some things on your own! There will be tons of girls there. I'm happy Mimi can take some time away from her writing and take us to Savannah. She says she needs a vacation!"

Mimi was the well-known children's mystery writer, Carole Marsh. Since Christina and Grant were older than their cousins, they often traveled with Mimi and Papa when Mimi researched her mystery books.

"Every time you go somewhere with Mimi, there's some kind of spooky mystery!" exclaimed Avery. "Isn't that how she gets all her ideas for the mystery books she writes?"

"Not this time," insisted Christina, patting her younger cousin's arm. "We have other things to do—and this trip is purely for fun! *No mysteries allowed*!"

As Christina closed her suitcase, her grandmother breezed into the room.

"Is everyone ready?" she asked, her shiny gold earrings swinging around her short, sassy, blond hair. "Papa's in the van and is ready to hit the road! Does anyone know where Grant is?"

"He was just here, Mimi," said Ella, throwing her little arms around Mimi.

Everyone looked around the bedroom.

"Yes, he was!" said Christina. "He just tornadoed my bed!"

Suddenly, Grant popped up from behind a chair. He clutched a box of mint cookies. His mouth was stuffed full, and chocolate cookie crumbs clung to his chin.

"Where did you get those?" cried Christina.

"Beshide urr bd," mumbled Grant, chewing. He gulped. "Beside your bed!"

Christina grabbed the empty cookie box and peered inside. "Empty!"

"Don't worry!" said Mimi. "There are plenty more where those came from. Let's go to Savannah!"

2

BOOM CHICKA BOOM!

"I said a Boom Chicka Boom
I said a Boom Chicka Boom
I said a Boom Chicka Rocka Chicka
Rocka Chicka Boom!"

The girls sang merrily in the back seats of the big black van as Papa drove down the highway, closer and closer to Savannah. Grant's chocolate-streaked chin flopped on his chest as he snored.

"Uh huh,
Oh yeah,
One more time 'Valley Girl' style!"

Grace sang loudly and pointed to Ella. Shy Ella sang softly.

"I said like Boom Chicka Boom,
I said a totally Boom Chicka Boom,

I said like Boom Chicka like Rocka Chicka like gag me with a spoon!"

Mimi laughed from the front seat. "I love it!" she exclaimed, turning around and clapping. "Now, how about a little Savannah history? We're nearly there!"

"I can tell them about James Oglethorpe, Mimi," said Christina. "He sailed from England with a group of settlers and founded Savannah in 1733. He had received a charter from the King of England to establish the Colony of Georgia. He built the colony on a bluff along the Savannah River. England wanted the town to act as a buffer between the Carolina colony to the north and Spanish Florida to the south. The settlers were supposed to produce silk, wine, and other things for the British Empire, too."

"You mean Georgia wasn't a state then?" asked Avery.

"No," said Christina. "That was before the Revolutionary War. There wasn't a United States yet."

"James Oglethorpe laid out the town in a pattern of wide streets, alleys, and squares," added Mimi. "Rectangular-shaped lots were marked off along the streets. He gave that property to the settlers to build their homes. Back then, they built small, wood houses. Much later, people built huge stone, stucco, and marble houses. Most of those houses still stand in the old part of Savannah."

"I love the squares," said Christina. "People call them 'Savannah's jewels.'"

"You'll see a lot of real characters walking around the streets of Savannah, too," added Mimi and laughed. "I'm sure you will see what I mean once we get there!"

"I think Savannah can be a little spooky," said Christina. "Mimi and I have been on a couple of ghost tours. People say most of the houses in Savannah are haunted. Except Mimi's, of course!"

"Whew! I'm glad of that," said Amber. "I can't wait to see the Juliette Gordon Low Birthplace again."

"What's a birthplace?" asked Ella.

"That's the place where someone is born," replied Mimi. "Juliette Gordon Low is the lady who started the Girl Scouts. She was born in a house in Savannah. It's now a National Historic Landmark! Hundreds of scouts and volunteers visit it every day. I see them getting their pictures taken in front of the house all the time."

"In fact, we have a surprise for you," said Christina. "Mimi and Papa's house is just a few blocks away from the Juliette Gordon Low Birthplace. We can walk over there tomorrow!"

"YEA!!" the girls cheered.

"Here we are!" said Papa. He turned the van to the right and exited off the highway into the historic district of Savannah. "There's the new Talmadge Memorial Bridge to the left. It crosses the Savannah River to South Carolina."

The girls sat forward in their seats and peered through the windows to see the gleaming white bridge in the distance. It looked like a large sailboat.

Papa maneuvered the van around Savannah's famous, sun-dappled squares. Enormous live oak trees spread limbs draped with feathery Spanish moss over the street and squares.

Mimi rolled her window down. "I love the perfumed smell of Savannah," she said. The fragrance of purple, white, pink, red, and yellow flowers mingled and drifted into the van.

Tall homes made from stucco, stone, and brick rose side by side up against the city sidewalks. Scrolled iron railings and fences decorated squares, monuments, fountains, and buildings.

"I feel like I'm at Disney World," said Grace, pressing her nose against the window. "And *that* must be one of the Savannah characters you were talking about, Mimi!"

All eyes turned to a scrawny old man in a shabby, black butler's uniform shuffling down the street. His longish, white-gray hair stuck out in all directions from under his black bowler hat.

"I've seen him around before," said Christina. "He's a Savannah regular. You see a lot of strange people on the streets every day."

"Let's call him Igor the Butler!" said Avery.

At that moment, the van pulled up to Mimi and Papa's house.

"Welcome to Savannah, girls!" Mimi announced.

SNORT!! From his seat in the back, Grant snorted and sat straight up. Rubbing his stomach, he blurted out, "Anyone got any cookies?"

3

WAVING GOODBYE TO BARGES!

Mimi, Papa, and the kids strolled out of the restaurant and onto River Street.

Grant rubbed his tummy and moaned, "I'm so full. I'm too full of shrimp to even eat a cookie crumb!"

"Thank goodness!" said Christina.

"That was delicious wild Georgia shrimp," said Mimi. "There's nothing like eating fresh shrimp caught in our coastal waters—it's just the best!"

River Street bustled with activity. Mimi, Papa, and the kids strolled down the cobblestone street past throngs of tourists. Clusters of blue, brown, green, and khaki scouting uniforms flitted from stores to restaurants to the river.

"Look at all the girls!" said Avery.

Grant was more interested in the uneven walkway beneath his feet. "Papa, it's like I'm walking on a bunch of big, fat, lumpy, bumpy rocks, but they're all stuck together," he said. "What is this stuff?"

"Cobblestones!" Papa replied. "In the old days, ships arrived at ports up and down the East Coast to load and unload cargo," he explained. "To keep a ship's weight stable, the crew added cobblestones for ballast. Then when they took on cargo, they would dump the ballast along the shoreline and the local residents used the cobblestones to pave streets."

"They look cool," Grant replied. "Wish I could pry a few out for my rock collection!"

"These have been here for hundreds of years, Grant—good luck!" said Papa.

"Just to break my shoe heels—or ankles!" Mimi worried, stumbling wobbly-legged over the breadloaf-sized stones.

A light breeze lifted whitecaps in the water. Barges, ships, and boats lined the wharfs along the Savannah River, which sparkled with red and gold light as the sun began to sink lower in the sky. The smell of warm pralines floated from nearby candy stores.

A tall, dapper man strolled past them wearing a blue seersucker suit and a yellow bow tie. He tipped his straw fedora at Mimi and Papa.

"Good evenin', y'all," he said with a thick Southern accent and a big smile.

"Good evening, Dan," said Mimi and Papa in unison.

Avery's blue eyes grew wide. "Do you know him, Mimi?" she asked after the man walked on.

"Of course," said Mimi. "That's Savannah Dan. He takes people on walking tours of Savannah. He tells lots of good stories about the town and folks who have lived here." Mimi suddenly stopped in front of a shop. "Ah, ha!" she exclaimed. "Here's a place you all will love!"

The sign above the door said Savannah's Candy Kitchen. Soon everyone was biting into sweet, sticky praline patties.

"These are so good!" said Grace, licking her fingers.

Grant picked chewy caramel from his teeth. "I like those peanut butter Girl Scout cookies better."

"I thought you liked the mint ones," said Christina.

"*All* cookies are delicious!" said Grant.

"How about the shortbread ones?" asked Amber. "Those are my favorite. A trefoil is the official emblem of the Girl Scouts."

"I'm not that big on eating trees," replied Grant. "But they'll do when everything else is gone."

"A trefoil isn't a tree, Grant," Amber explained. "The symbol comes from a leaf having three leaflets. The three trefoil leaves represent the three-fold Girl Scout promise— 'To serve God and my country, to help people at all times, and to live by the Girl Scout Law.'"

"Try a little peanut butter on them!" whispered Amber.

"Grant, we better get home and get in bed," said Papa. "We have to get on the shrimp boat at the break of dawn."

"Dawn breaks?" asked Grant.

"Every day!" insisted Papa.

"I'm tired, too," said Mimi. "You girls can keep sightseeing. Just get home by dark."

When the others headed off, the five girls continued along River Street, tripping on cobblestones and acting silly. They gave the scouting sign with their right hand to other scouts they spotted along the way.

"Here's one of my favorite places," said Christina, when they reached the end of the walkway. "And it's one of my favorite Savannah stories."

She led the way past some hedges and into a small park alongside the river. They followed a brick walkway to the statue of a young woman facing the water. She held her arms up waving a large handkerchief. A dog stood by her side, looking out at the water along with her.

"It's the Waving Girl," Christina explained.

"Who is she waving to?" asked Avery.

"Her name is Florence Martus," replied Christina. "A long time ago, she decided to greet all the ships that entered or left Savannah Harbor. She waved a handkerchief by day and a lantern by night. The legend says that she did not miss a single ship between

1887 and 1931. Ship captains always looked for her. She became famous around the world! After she retired, they erected this statue in her honor."

"Why did she do it?" asked Grace. "That's a lot of waving!"

"Maybe she was lonesome," guessed Christina. "She lived with her brother on Elba Island, a tiny island in the river near the Atlantic Ocean. He was the lighthouse keeper. One legend says she greeted ships because she fell in love with a sailor. She wanted to be sure he found her when he returned. But there's no proof to that."

"Too bad," said Amber. "That's so romantic!"

"And sad," added Avery.

As they headed toward the river, an ancient, wrinkled old lady popped from behind the hedge and ambled toward them. She was dressed in a long, flowing, gray dress. A tattered, gray fringed shawl covered her hunched back. A gray satin ribbon held back long hair, the same color as Spanish moss. The bright spot in her drab appearance was the large sweetgrass basket of yellow daisies she carried in the crook of her arm. Ella gave her a sweet, two-front-teeth-missing grin. The lady nodded shyly and slowly shuffled by, saying not a word.

"She was REALLY old!" said Avery.

"I think I've seen her before," Christina mused. She turned back to the riverside. "I think this is a good place for our barges ceremony."

The sun sank lower as the girls walked to the water's edge. They each pulled a piece of tree bark, a stick of gum, and a candle from their backpacks. In unison, they chewed the gum for a few seconds. Then, each girl took the gum from her mouth and stuck it on her tree bark. Next, she stuck the candle into the gum.

Christina flicked a lighter and lit their candles one by one. All together, they slid their "barges" into the river and sang. The girls clasped hands as they watched their barges sail away into the setting sun.

"We're starting a new adventure," said Christina. She loved working with younger scouts.

"Wow," said Amber. "That may be the best barges ceremony I've ever done!"

When they could no longer see their barges, the group solemnly turned and headed toward the steep steps to Bay Street.

When Avery picked her backpack up off the grass, she spotted a small piece of paper with a faded shamrock and scrawled handwriting on it. "Listen to this!" she said.

> Barges sail far away.
> Enjoy Savannah the
> scouting way!

Just then, the girls heard a high-pitched giggle.

"Why are you laughing?" Avery asked, turning to Ella.

"I didn't laugh!" said Ella. "Honest!"

The five girls looked around to see who else heard Avery read the note. But there was no one—no one at all.

That's creepy, thought Avery, stuffing the note in her backpack. *Why would someone giggle at this note? And where did this note come from?*

4

DEAD INDIANS AND SHRIEKS!

Dusk was melting into night as the girls strolled through the historic district. Gaslights cast a soft glow on the cobblestone streets. The chatter of tourists filled the air.

"See?" said Avery to Christina, in an "I told you so!" voice. "Everywhere you go with Mimi, you find a mystery."

Christina laughed. "I don't think there's a mystery here, Avery," she said. "It's just a piece of paper a scout dropped. Look, I have to go back to Mimi's now. I have to plan my research schedule for tomorrow."

"Can we walk around some of the squares on our way to Mimi's?" asked Avery.

"Sure," replied Christina. "Amber, you are in charge. You all stay together and be at Mimi's before it gets too dark."

"On my honor!" they said in unison.

"Do you remember how to get back?" Christina asked, as she strolled off.

"Be prepared!" said Amber, holding up the map in her guidebook.

"Be prepared!" said Avery, pressing the GPS icon on her iPod.

"Be prepared!" said Grace. She dug into her backpack and yanked out a flashlight.

"Be prepared!" said Ella, tugging a few cookies from her backpack. Everyone giggled and waved goodbye to Christina.

Arm in arm, the girls strolled up Savannah's famous Bull Street. They stopped at Johnson Square, the first square James Oglethorpe laid out in 1733.

"This square was the center of daily life in the earliest days of the colony," Amber read from her guidebook. "The statue is Nathanael Greene. He was a general of the Continental Army in the Revolutionary War."

It was already growing darker as the girls wandered out of the spooky square.

Avery followed their progress on her iPod. "I love the way the little blue dot moves as we move," she said. "It's like we're being followed by a tiny blue ghost."

"What square is this?" Ella asked as they approached another park in the middle of the street.

"Wright Square," replied Amber.

"That's wrong," argued Avery, staring at the iPod screen.

"No—it's 'Wright!'" insisted Ella, and the other girls laughed.

Benches and gaslights surrounded the square. Huge live oak trees created a spooky canopy over it. In the middle stood a large monument glowing from the spotlights aimed its way. The four girls walked around a hedge and stopped near the monument.

"OOOOOH!" said Amber, reading her guidebook. "They used to hang people here. There was a gallows for public hangings right here."

"That's creepy," said Avery, looking over her shoulder.

"This historical marker says an Indian named Tomochichi is buried here, too," said Grace.

"What?" asked Ella. "Hung? Buried? Dead people? Ghosts?" Goosebumps popped up on her tiny arms.

"Tomochichi was the chief of the Yamacraw Indians," Grace continued. "He became friends with the colonists. General Oglethorpe helped carry his body here to be buried."

"That boulder marks his grave," said Amber, pointing to a large rock. The girls gathered around it.

"Do you think there are ghosts here?" said Ella, slipping her hand into Avery's.

"There *aren't* any ghosts!" said Grace. "I *don't believe* in ghosts!"

"But Savannah is the most haunted town in America," said Amber. "It says so right here in this guidebook!"

Just then, the girls spotted a swaying lantern slowly moving toward them. It came closer, closer, closer, and closer. And then the girls started to shriek!

5

THE BLOODY GALLOWS!

A tall, thin woman appeared at the edge of the square. She carried the lantern high over her head. She wore a long, black dress and cape and an old fashioned, black satin bonnet. A group of tourists with cameras followed her.

The woman stopped abruptly when she came face to face with the four girls. The glow from the lantern cast shadows and reddish streaks of light on her long, thin, witch-like face.

"Sorry I startled you, my dears," she said in a deep, dramatic voice, not really sounding sorry at all. She swung around slowly, holding the lamp high over the crowd behind her.

"This is Wright Square," the lady in black said. "A coastal Georgia legend says that Spanish moss will *not* grow where innocent blood was spilled. And as you can see, it will not grow in Wright Square."

The woman held her lamp higher. She turned full circle to cast slivers of amber light on the live oak trees that enclosed the square.

"There is *noooooooo* Spanish moss here, you see," the lady said slowly, "because Alice Riley was hung here for a crime she committed in self-defense. The young woman murdered a wealthy but cruel man who harmed her. But no one believed her story. They only saw her crime. Now, people claim to see a young woman dressed in rags running through Wright Square screaming for her baby."

Ella clutched Avery's arm. Her eyes grew wide and her little knees shivered.

"Many people believe it is Alice," said the lady, her eyes flashing with the glow of flickering lantern light. "People claim they've seen her sitting right under that tree where the gallows once stood!"

The lady in black waved her lantern at a live oak tree right beside the girls. They gasped.

"She is crying!" the lady in black sobbed. "If you approach her, she vanishes! People have tried to prove why *noooooooo* Spanish moss will grow in the trees on Wright Square but there is *noooooooo* other reason for it."

The woman's voice grew low and sinister. "As I said before, Spanish moss will *not grooooowwwww* where innocent blood has been spilled."

The woman spun on her tall black heels and stalked out of the square. The tourists followed, nervously chattering and giggling.

The girls collapsed on a park bench.

"I *still* don't believe in ghosts," said Grace, "but that was spooky!" Just then, she spied a piece of paper with a faded shamrock on it lying beneath the bench. She picked it up and read it aloud:

> ## Juliette, oh Juliette, where were thou born?

"HeeeHeeeHeeee!!!" A muffled, high giggle came from behind the hedge. The girls clung tightly to each other.

Suddenly, Savannah Dan appeared, heading home from his last tour of the day. "You girls might want to get home now," he admonished them. "It's getting way too late for young ladies to be scampering around Savannah."

Still clutching each other's hands, the girls made a dash for Mimi's house. They knew that while it might be too late for girls, it was possible that the ghosts were just getting warmed up!

6

IS IT A MYSTERY OR JUST CREEPY?

Sun streamed through Mimi's kitchen windows. All the girls chatted as they sat in their pajamas at the breakfast table. Shrimp and grits, a Savannah favorite, filled their plates. Mimi set a platter stacked with buttery French toast in the center of the table, and the girls *oohed* and *aahed*.

"When did Papa and Grant leave this morning, Mimi?" asked Ella.

"Very early," replied Mimi. "You should have heard Grant. He didn't realize he had to get up before sunrise. He grumbled all the way through breakfast!"

"He probably grumbled all the way to Tie-Bee Island!" said Christina, reaching for the jam.

"I heard Papa say Tybee Island is a barrier island," said Amber. "What does that mean?"

"A barrier island is an island that buffers, or protects, the coast from storms," said Mimi. "There are about 15 major barrier islands strung along Georgia's coast, plus a lot of smaller islands. Marshes and waterways separate them from the mainland. Some of the islands are wild and beautiful and mostly in their natural state. Others, like Tybee, have beach houses, hotels, restaurants, and pirate parades!" Mimi picked up her coffee cup. "I think I'll go out and enjoy the garden."

As soon as Mimi vanished out the French doors, Avery said, "Look what we found at Wright Square last night!" She handed Christina the second note.

"Interesting!" said Christina.

"We think someone is leaving clues for us," said Avery.

"Or *some thing*!" said Amber.

"Avery, don't worry," Christina begged. "This isn't a mystery. I think it's a Girl Scout scavenger hunt. You girls are somehow finding clues meant for someone else!"

"*I don't know,*" said Avery, frowning.

"Well, then," said Christina, "this note seems to want us to go to where Juliette Gordon Low was born. So let's get going! By the way, people claim they have seen ghosts there! You never know, maybe a ghost will leave you another clue!" Christina winked at Ella.

Ella gulped and grimaced.

"Well, I'm not afraid of ghosts," said Grace grumpily.

"I thought you said you didn't believe in ghosts, Grace!" Amber reminded her.

"Well, if there WERE ghosts, I wouldn't be afraid of them!" Grace said, folding her arms stubbornly across her chest.

Christina laughed. "I'm going to take a shower, girls," she said. "We'll go to the Juliette Gordon Low Birthplace when everyone is ready!"

The girls jumped up and started clearing the table.

Christina may not think we have a mystery, but I do, thought Avery, shuddering. *And, if it's NOT a mystery, it sure is something creepy!!*

7

GET LOW!

The girls entered the Juliette Gordon Low Birthplace through a street-level entrance off Oglethorpe Street.

"Juliette, oh, Juliette, HERE is where thou were born!" cried Grace, flinging her arms wide open.

"Grace, you should be an actress some day," said Avery as Christina opened the door.

"That's what my mother says!" said Grace, giving a bow.

Inside the home, a tour was getting underway.

"Come on in!" said the tour guide. "We have lots of Girl Scouts today. I guess everyone is arriving in Savannah for the Camporee."

Green, brown, blue, and khaki clad girls filled the hall of the old Victorian home. Christina, Avery, Ella, Amber, and Grace huddled close to their tour guide.

"We are really excited to see Daisy's home!" said Avery.

"Daisy would have loved to see this many girls visiting her home," said the tour guide. "As you all know, this is the birthplace of Juliette Gordon Low, founder of the Girl Scouts. Her family and friends called her Daisy."

Ella smiled and touched her daisy headband.

"We call this house The Birthplace, but it is much older than Daisy," said the guide. "It was built by the Wayne family in 1821. Ten years later, Daisy's grandfather bought it. Daisy's father grew up here. After he married Daisy's mother, they lived here for the rest of their lives."

The tour guide pointed to a photo of the Gordon family. "Daisy was the second oldest of five children," she said. "It was a very lively family. One family story says that Daisy's mother, who was called Nellie, slid all the way down this curved staircase when she was 82 years old!"

"I'm sure glad Grant isn't here," said Christina.

"He couldn't resist!" Avery agreed.

"Daisy lived here until she married William Low in 1886," the tour guide continued. "Then, she moved into the Low family home, which is also here in Savannah."

"I heard that Daisy couldn't hear very well," said Amber.

"That's very true!" said the guide. "Daisy lost some of her hearing in one ear from an illness. And then a terrible thing happened on her wedding day! As was the tradition, wedding guests threw rice at Daisy and her new husband after the wedding to wish them good luck. But it wasn't good luck for Daisy! Do you know what happened?"

"Yes!" replied Amber. "A grain of rice got stuck in her other ear!"

"Ouch!" cried Grace.

"You are absolutely right!" said the guide. "And that ear became so infected that eventually Daisy became deaf. After that, she often said that when somebody told her NO— she just told them she couldn't hear them!"

Everyone laughed.

"The Girl Scouts organization purchased this home in 1953," said the tour guide. "It was renovated to look like it did in 1886 when Daisy was making preparations for her wedding. Many of the furnishings you see belonged to the Gordon family. This artwork was actually created by Juliette herself!"

"Wow!" said Grace. "She was a good artist!"

The girls stopped in the library to gaze at a portrait of Juliette when she was a young woman. A stunning young woman sat before them in a flowing pink dress, her brown hair and dark eyes sparkling in the soft lighting.

"She was really pretty," said Avery.

Ella nodded, her eyes fixed on the portrait. "She looks so nice and calm," she added.

"Listen to what this says about ghosts at the Birthplace," said Amber, looking at her guidebook. "People have heard the sound of piano playing in the house—when no one was here!"

"I saw a piano in the formal parlor!" said Christina.

"Do you actually have to have a piano to hear a ghost playing a piano?" asked Grace, scrunching up her eyebrows and cocking her head.

Amber jabbed Grace with her elbow.

"People also say they've seen Daisy's father running down the stairs, calling for her mother," said Amber. "AND, they say that Daisy's grandmother and mother have been known to haunt the house, too!"

"Well, let's keep on the lookout!" said Grace, rolling her eyes. Still, she peeked behind a door before she quickly scurried into the next room.

Avery thought about the two notes written on paper with faded shamrocks tucked away in her backpack. She listened for the familiar giggle. But all she could hear were giggling girls—gobs and gobs of them!

8

GIGGLES IN THE GARDEN!

"Hey, girls," Christina called, "this is a famous gate. Let me take your picture beside it."

Avery, Ella, Grace, and Amber lined up beside an iron gate in the garden of the Juliette Gordon Low Birthplace. The elaborate gate was shaped in the Girl Scout trefoil symbol.

"We need your picture, too, Christina!" said Avery.

"Here, let's get the cousins together!" said Grace, taking Christina's camera.

Avery, Ella, and Christina hugged and laughed as Grace clicked away with her digital camera.

Amber plopped down on a bench and opened a brochure the tour guide had given her. "I came here with my Brownie troop once," she said. "We took a class where we learned to play old-fashioned games like Daisy played. We dressed up in bonnets and long dresses with hoop skirts."

"I came here with my troop, too," said Christina. "We learned to weave and spin in one class. On another day, we did sculpting and artwork. See that porch over there? That's where we had our pinning ceremony."

"Ella, you would like this class," said Amber. "You get to make paper dolls like Daisy did when she was little."

"OOHH!" said Ella, her eyes wide. She loved paper dolls.

"This class looks like fun," said Grace. "You learn how to do calisthenics, marching, and Morse code signaling. That's what the first scouts learned!"

Christina glanced at her watch. "I almost forgot," she said. "I need to pick up information about my project. I better scoot! I'll text you later and we can meet up."

After Christina left, Avery, Ella, Grace, and Amber wandered through the garden with its spiky century plants and wisteria-laden fence.

"I want to come here with my troop someday," said Ella wistfully.

Amber stopped in front of a bed of tall, colorful flowers. "Listen to this!" she said. "Juliette Gordon Low's great-grandmother was captured by Indians when she was little!"

All of a sudden, the girls heard a high-pitched giggle. They glanced around.

"Here it is!" whispered Ella.

A piece of paper floated through the air. It landed on the garden path right in front of the girls.

Ella snatched it up as the girls huddled around her. Amber read aloud:

Forsyth Park is where
they like to play,
when lively scouts
come this way!

"Well, OK! There's no doubt about it now," Amber whispered. "*Somebody* is definitely following us! Three notes—and to me, you've officially got a mystery!"

9

F-F-F-FORSYTH F-F-F-FOUNTAIN!

Avery, Ella, Amber and Grace sat on the grass at Forsyth Park. The majestic old fountain stood nearby, spraying streams of water in every direction. Huge live oak trees, draped in Spanish moss, framed the fountain and formed a canopy over their heads.

"You hold one palm down," said Grace to Ella, "and the other palm up. Then, while we sing 'Down by the Banks,' we go around the circle hitting each other's hand. The last one to get their hand hit is out!"

The girls began to sing.

"Down by the banks of the hanky panky
Where the bullfrogs jump from bank to
banky
With an eeps iipes oupss uppss

and an uflop a dilly and a uunflop flop
pepsi cola ginger ale
ginger ale ginger ginger ale ginger ale
pepsi cola ginger ale 7-up 7-up – up
You're OUT!!"

"Oh, man!" said Grace. "I'm out. OK, go again!"

Just then, a troop of Girl Scouts walked up.

"Can we play?" asked one of the girls.

"You sure can!" said Grace, plopping back down. "This game is more fun to play with more people!"

The girls played the game over and over again, until they were exhausted. Before long, they were giggling and chattering like old friends.

"Time to go!" called a troop leader to their new friends.

"We're headed to the Juliette Gordon Low Birthplace," said one of the girls.

"We went this morning," said Avery. "It was great fun!"

All the girls opened their backpacks and began exchanging SWAPS.

"Listen, listen!" said Ella, excitedly. "I can say this really, really fast! Special Whatchamacallits Affectionately Pinned Somewhere or Shared With A Pal!"

Ella sputtered out the words three times in a row at breakneck speed. Everyone applauded and hugged her. Then, the troop waved goodbye and hurried off.

Avery, Ella, Grace, and Amber walked over to the fountain and leaned against the railing.

"Oh, I can feel the spray," said Amber. "It feels good. I wish we could get in!"

"Well, that new clue was right," said Avery. "Forsyth Park is where Girl Scouts like to play!"

"No new clues here!" said Ella, relieved.

"I'm a little disappointed," admitted Avery. "No new clues and no giggling ghosts!"

"That's what we can call it!" said Ella. "The Giggling Ghost!"

"Good name!" said Grace. "But I STILL don't believe in ghosts!"

The four girls locked arms and skipped out of Forsyth Park. But every once in a while,

Avery glanced over her shoulder to make sure no one was following them.

Of course, someone WAS!

10

DO GHOSTS EAT CUPCAKES?

"This might be the best red velvet cupcake I ever ate," said Ella, licking cream cheese frosting off her fingers.

The girls sat in ice cream parlor chairs around a small table at Mabel Francis Potter's Cupcake Emporium.

"I've never heard of so many flavors," said Avery, biting into her key lime cupcake. "What kind did you get, Grace?"

"It's chocolate with peanut butter frosting," replied Grace. "My absolute favorite!" She tipped back in her chair and rubbed her tummy contentedly.

"I went out on a limb with this almond cupcake with pistachio frosting," said Amber. "But it's pretty tasty."

"Ella, you've got frosting on your nose!" Avery said, and swiped at her sister's button nose.

Amber's phone rang. "Hey, Christina!" she said. "We're eating yummy cupcakes! Yes. OK. I'll tell Avery!"

"Christina wants us to come to something called Massie School," said Amber. "She said to put it in your GPS locator."

Fifteen minutes later, the girls paraded into the old Massie Common School, Savannah's first public school. Tourists and more Girl Scouts roamed around the lobby.

"Isn't this a neat old place?" Christina greeted them.

"It says here that the school opened in 1856," said Amber, reading her guidebook. "That's before the Civil War. And it stayed open for about 120 years."

"Now it's a museum," said Christina. "It has some cool exhibits about Savannah."

The girls followed her into a room featuring a 3-D model of early Savannah.

"Look at this," Christina said, pointing to the model. "It covers the entire Historic District."

"Can you see Mimi's house?" asked Avery.

"It's here," said Christina, pointing to a brick building on the model, "the old Derst bread factory."

"There's Wright Square and Johnson Square, where we went the first evening," said Amber.

"Here's Forsyth Park," said Grace. "And the Savannah River, of course!"

"Where is the Juliette Gordon Low Birthplace?" asked Ella.

Christina pointed to a building in the model.

"It's like a dollhouse," said Ella, admiring the large display.

"Let's go upstairs," said Christina. "You'll like it, too; it's really cool."

The girls scampered up a curved wooden staircase to an old-time schoolroom.

"Wow!" said Grace. "Schoolrooms sure used to be brown and boring!"

"Yeah," said Amber. "It looks so different from our colorful classrooms today."

Avery sat down at an old wooden desk. "What's this?" she said, pointing to a hole in the upper right corner of the desk.

"It's an inkwell," said Christina. "That's where you put a jar of ink."

Ella looked confused.

"You had to dip a pen in ink so you could write, Ella," Christina explained. "Only boys would sometimes stick the girls' pigtails in the ink instead!"

"Oh!" said Ella, grabbing her hair.

"We're lucky we didn't live back then," said Avery.

"Oh, I would love to have lived in the past!" said Christina. "Just me, history, and ghosts!"

"Maybe you could have been one of the first Girl Scouts!" said Amber.

"That sure would have been fun," said Christina, heading back down the stairs.

The girls walked around the exhibits some more, looking at old maps, photos, and historic artifacts.

"People think James Oglethorpe used this compass when he laid out the city of Savannah," said Christina.

"You've got James Oglethorpe on the brain, girl!" said Grace, shaking her head.

"I've got Savannah on the brain," said Christina. "I love it! I'm so glad Mimi has a house here, and I hope to go to architecture school at SCAD, the Savannah College of Art and Design. I've got to get back to researching now. I sure wish I'd asked you guys to bring me a cupcake!"

Ella's face lit up. She reached into her backpack. "I didn't forget you, Christina," she said. "Do a good turn daily!"

"Oh, Ella, you sweetheart!" said Christina, giving her cousin a big hug. "My favorite: chocolate with raspberry icing!"

Ella beamed.

"Now that I've seen this 3-D version of Savannah," said Grace, "I want to explore some more of the city squares! Let's get going!"

"Whoops!" said Amber as they walked out the door. "I left my guidebook somewhere."

The girls dashed back inside and looked everywhere. Finally, Amber discovered it lying on a bench.

"I don't remember putting it there," she said. "What's this?"

Sticking between the pages was a note—another clue!

The girls gathered around as Amber read.

Once a little girl named Daisy liked to roam the squares like crazy!

Suddenly, they heard high-pitched giggling from behind an old-time blackboard, dusty with a film of ghostly white chalk. Avery crept over and peeked around the corner, but all she could see were Girl Scouts, and more Girl Scouts, and more Girl Scouts!

11

BROWNIES, ANYONE?

Gray clouds rolled into Savannah, pushing the blue sky out to sea.

"Oh, no!" cried Avery. "Where is the sun going? We've got places to go and things to see!"

"Guess we better get moving, then!" said Grace.

Avery, Ella, Amber, and Grace linked arms and skipped off to explore more of Savannah.

The town was bursting with happy girls now. The Camporee was just a couple of days away. Clumps of blue, brown, green, and khaki buzzed like honey bees from place to place. The background noise was constant chatter with an occasional scream or shout as old friends were spotted. Silvery, girly laughter floated through the air.

The four friends stopped in front of a park near the heart of the historic district. A sign said "Chippewa Square."

Amber flipped though her guidebook.

"OK, Chip-a-wa Square," she said slowly. "Here it is! This square is named for the Battle of Chippewa during the War of 1812. And guess what? There's a statue of Christina's hero here!"

The girls walked toward a large, bronze statue in the middle of the square.

General James Oglethorpe loomed over them. He stood on a tall, marble pedestal perched atop a wide concrete base. His left hand was placed firmly on one hip. In his other hand, he held a sword, the tip of which he planted into the ground. Four lions guarded the corners of the monument base. General Oglethorpe looked straight ahead with a steely gaze.

"He looks ferocious!" said Grace.

"He looks like he's saying, 'I'm here to stay!'" added Avery.

"I think that's what he's telling the Spanish," said Amber. "It says here that he is facing south toward Georgia's one-time enemy, Spanish Florida."

All around the monument, tourists snapped photos.

"Where's your camera, Avery?" asked Ella. "Let's take a picture in front of him for Christina."

"Hi! My name is Brianna Brown," said a young girl standing nearby. "Would you like me to take a picture of all of you?"

"Thanks!" said Avery, handing her the camera.

The four friends lined up in front of the base of the statue.

"Say, 'cookies!'" said Brianna.

The girls grinned and yelled, "COOOOKKKIES!"

Brianna handed the camera back to Avery. Then she and Avery exchanged the special scout handshake.

"What a great picture!" said Avery, looking at her iPod. "I'll text it to Christina right now!"

Grace cocked her head and put her hand on her hips. "I just thought of something," she said. "I don't get it! How come General Oglethorpe's statue is not in Oglethorpe Square?"

"I saw something about that," said Amber, flipping through her guidebook. "Here it is. Savannah's squares and monuments don't match. The General Oglethorpe monument is in Chippewa Square rather than Oglethorpe Square. The Count Pulaski Monument is in Monterey Square rather than Pulaski Square. And the General Nathanael Greene Monument is in Johnson Square instead of Greene Square."

"Huh?!" said Ella.

"That's too confusing," said Grace, shaking her head. "They messed this thing up. They need to fix it! How am I supposed to remember this so I can tell my mama what I saw?"

She flopped down on a bench beside General Oglethorpe's statue, fished out a new box of Girl Scout cookies from her backpack, and opened it.

"*WHERE DID MY COOKIES GO?*" yelled Grace.

She turned the box upside down. It was empty!

The girls looked at each other and said in unison, "Grant!!!"

"Even when Grant isn't here, he's here!!" said Avery.

Grace sighed and shoved the empty box back into her backpack. She looked up at General Oglethorpe's statue and noticed a familiar looking piece of paper stuck to the tip of his sword.

She jumped up. "What's this?" she said, climbing up the monument base and plucking it off.

The girls gathered around her to read:

Little Brownies come and go, but they always eat ice cream at Leopold's!

Just as they anticipated, the girls heard that familiar giggle.

"Where is it coming from?" said Avery, racing around the statute. "All I see are girls everywhere!"

"I still don't believe in ghosts," said Grace, "but this clue has a good idea!"

Grace handed the new clue to Avery, who entered *LEOPOLD'S* into her GPS locator.

"Let's go!" Avery said, and she began to run.

As they left the square, they heard the strange, high giggle behind them yet again. Avery spun around to look back. But no one was there. *At least, no one she could see!*

12

CARRIAGES AND TOOTHLESS GRINS!

The pink neon Leopold's Ice Cream sign glowed eerily in the late afternoon gloom. But inside, the cheerful ice cream parlor, with its movie theater motif, was crammed with Girl Scouts. Scouts leaned against the long, black marble counters. Scout noses pressed against the glass ice cream freezers. Scout arms and legs hung over every chair and marble-topped table. Leopold servers in red aprons scooped ice cream from bins as quickly as possible. But more scouts kept coming!

"Avery," said Grace, tipping precariously on her chair, "I think EVERYONE got the same clue about coming to Leopold's. I'm not sure we're anything special to this ghost."

"You've got a good point," said Avery, nodding her head. "I think half the Girl Scouts in America are right here right now!"

Grace pushed her long stemmed spoon deep into a tall soda glass. "I'm sure happy to have this Thin Mint Cookies and Cream ice cream float. It kind of makes up for that rascally Grant eating my Thin Mint cookies!"

Ice cream drooled down Ella's mouth as she laughed. "Your face was so funny when you realized that cookie box was empty!"

Avery wiped the drool from Ella's chin.

Amber slurped the last melted clumps of her Savannah Smiles ice cream sundae. "Not to change the subject," she said. "But do they make these ice cream flavors just to honor Girl Scouts?"

"Christina says they do," answered Avery. "I can't decide which one is my favorite!"

Avery checked the time on her iPod. "OK, Mimi should be right out front like she promised. She's taking us shopping!"

Just then, some Girl Scouts, standing outside Leopold's waiting to get in, began to chant!

We are the Girl Scouts
The mighty, mighty Girl Scouts
Everywhere we go
People want to know
Who we are
Where we're from
So we tell them

Avery, Ella, Grace, and Amber joined the chant as they finished up their ice cream treats and scampered out the door onto Broughton Street where Mimi waited.

"It looks like we might get some rain!" said Mimi. She zipped up her red rain jacket. "Do you girls have an umbrella?"

"Be prepared!" said the girls in unison as they each pulled a different color umbrella from their backpacks.

"I should have known!" said Mimi with a laugh. She popped open her red parasol umbrella she'd gotten from her favorite store—Paris Market.

Mimi and the girls bumped into other tourists wandering in and out of every store that looked like fun. And they *all* looked like fun!

The girls bought souvenirs at Mack's 5 & 10. They gazed at the lighted paper stars hanging from the ceiling at Parker's. They gobbled hot dogs at the Soda Pop Shoppe. They looked at clothes and shoes and books and toys. And as they walked and shopped, they met other girls who were just as excited to be in Savannah as they were.

"Can we take a carriage ride, Mimi?" asked Grace. She began waving her arms as an empty carriage approached them.

"Of course!" said Mimi. "We're lucky to find an empty one!"

"I love this!" said Ella, as the horse clomped down the street and the carriage swayed. "I feel like Cinderella or a princess."

"All the usual characters are out on the street today!" noted Mimi, with a wave or two.

Savannah Dan tipped his hat and waved back.

Just then, Avery spotted the old butler. *It's Igor,* she thought. *Why is he peeking around that lamppost? For some reason, he really gives me the creeps! I wonder if HE has a high-pitched giggle?*

All at once, Igor smiled a wide, toothless grin at her and slowly waved his hand.

Avery felt a tingle go up her spine. *And a shiver go down.*

13

HORNSWOGGLED BY A PIRATE!

Rain pelted the windows as Mimi, Papa, Grant, and the girls sat in The Pirates' House restaurant. Built in 1753, a block from the Savannah River, the rickety-looking, gray wooden building was once an old pirate inn.

"You know," said Papa, "bloodthirsty pirates and sailors of the high seas used to drink and eat in these very rooms!"

Grant brandished an imaginary sword. "I'd like to see that, matey!" he cried.

"ARRRGGGHHH!" shouted a "real" pirate walking past their table. He sported long black dreadlocks and a red bandana around his head. "Maybe we can arrange that, me bucko!"

"That's OK! N-n-n-not today, Captain!" said Grant, putting down his imaginary sword and picking up his spoon. He slumped over his plate and tried to be invisible.

"How was the shrimp boat trip?" asked Christina.

"I NEVER want to see another shrimp in my life!" said Grant.

Christina dipped a plump, wild Georgia shrimp into cocktail sauce and plunked it into her mouth.

"Deeeelicious!" she said to Grant as she chewed.

"UGH!" said Grant, making a gagging noise. "You wouldn't eat that if you saw what I saw today! These men pull them out of the ocean in big nets. They are soooooo slimy. They have little, beady black eyes. And they have skinny, creepy, red legs. And their antennae stick up and twitch." He skittered and squirmed in his chair, waving his arms like giant shrimp antennae.

"STOP! STOP!" squealed Ella, Avery, Amber, and Grace.

Christina merely plopped another juicy shrimp into her mouth and smacked her lips.

"Tell us some of The Pirates' House's famous ghost stories," said Mimi to the waiter, as he filled their water glasses.

"We have plenty of ghostly laughter, strange footsteps, and objects that move around here, that's for sure!" replied the waiter in a mysterious voice. "Some old salts and VERY dead pirates haunt these rooms!"

"Like who?" asked Grace, curious.

"Old Captain Flint, who buried the enormous treasure on Treasure Island, died in an upstairs room," said the waiter. "His faithful first mate, Billy Bones, was at his side when he muttered his last words."

"What did he say?" whispered Avery.

The waiter leaned toward the table. "Darby, bring aft the rum!" said the waiter in his best pirate voice. "People swear they've seen his ghost here on moonless nights."

"Isn't there an old tunnel here that leads to the edge of the river?" asked Mimi.

"There is," said the waiter. "It's pretty eerie."

"What was it for?" asked Amber. Her blue eyes were glued to the waiter's face.

"Sailing was dangerous work," said the waiter. "Many times, crews needed more men to work on seagoing ships. It was a common practice to fill a man with rum until he passed out. Then, the sailors would haul him to a docked sailing ship at the end of that tunnel. The next thing that guy knew, he was swabbing a deck and headed for Singapore."

"Wow!" said Grant, scrunching down in his seat. "I wouldn't want to do that."

"What?!" cried Papa. "Not want to be hornswoggled and kidnapped to sail the high seas for a merry—*but short*—life?"

The kids all giggled.

Mimi could see that school and home suddenly sounded like very safe ports to them.

The waiter eyed Papa suspiciously. "No one," said the waiter, "would want to eat hardtack filled with weevils, get scurvy and have their nose fall off, or be keelhauled across a barnacled bottom..."

"Uh, thank you!" interrupted Mimi. "I believe we'll have our check now, please."

"I read *Treasure Island* by Robert Louis Stevenson last summer," said Amber. "I remember Captain Flint."

"Let's look around," said Christina. "There are a bunch of rooms here with old photos and pages from the book that show those great old Andrew Wyeth pirate paintings. Mimi has one on her bathroom wall!"

"I'm staying here," said Grant. "I don't want to end up on a boat to Sink-A-Poo!"

The five girls explored the many nooks and crannies in The Pirates' House. They gazed at faded, brittle old prints and inspected treasure maps. They pondered the fact that girls like Mary Reid and Anne Bonney had also been pirates.

"Look at these old steps," said Avery, spying a hidden staircase.

The girls peered down into a dirty, well-worn stairway that spiraled down into the ground.

"I bet these are the steps that lead to the tunnel!" said Avery. She tiptoed down a few of them.

"Don't go down there, Avery," said Christina, holding Ella's hand.

"Just a little ways, Christina," said Avery, stepping down another step.

Grace whipped a flashlight out of her backpack and leapt down the steps with Avery. She waved the flashlight all around the tunnel's dirty, worn brick walls.

"I wonder if Captain Flint ever went down these steps?" Amber asked.

Just as Avery took another step down into the tunnel, she heard something that made her freeze in her footsteps.

A giggling sound echoed from deep in the tunnel.

Avery took another step down with Grace and Amber right behind her.

Ella pulled on Christina's arm, and the two girls started to follow.

"BOO!!!!" screamed Grant at the top of his lungs from behind them.

All five girls shrieked and ran back up the spiral staircase. Grant roared with laughter as the girls raced back to their table.

"Did you really think," he chortled, "that I was afraid a pirate would kidnap me and put me on a boat?!" He laughed hysterically.

As everyone left the restaurant, Ella handed a piece of paper to Avery.

"I found it on the floor back there," she whispered. "In the staircase."

Avery silently read the note:

> Back when Girl Scouts were very new, they would meet in this house, too!

"What is it?" asked Christina, watching Avery tilt her head, listening.

"It's our giggling ghost," whispered Avery, shuddering and glancing behind her as she walked out of The Pirates' House.

Surely their "giggling ghost" was not a pirate? Surely?!

14

S' MORE GHOSTS, PLEASE!

Mimi's house was dark except for the glow from the brick fireplace and an occasional flash of lightning. The pajama-clad girls huddled around the hearth roasting marshmallows. Rain splattered on the windowpanes, and the old oaks and palm trees rustled in the wind.

"I always say a dark room and a fireplace can be Plan B for a good campfire!" said Mimi. "Are you ready for your graham crackers?"

The girls were making s'mores, a favorite treat. Mimi handed each of them two graham crackers with a chocolate bar in between them. The girls placed a hot, golden brown roasted marshmallow on one chocolate-covered graham cracker and topped it with the second.

"Oh, I want some more!" said Ella, licking her ooey gooey fingers.

"Did you know that 'some more' is how 's'mores' got its name?" asked Christina.

"What?" said Ella, sticking another marshmallow on a coat hanger.

"S'more is a contraction of the phrase 'some more,'" replied Christina. "A lady named Loretta Scott Crew came up with the recipe. She made s'mores by a campfire with some scouts back in 1927. That's almost 100 years ago! The recipe was printed in a book called *Tramping and Trailing with the Girl Scouts.*"

"I can't believe Grant didn't want some of these!" said Avery.

"I think Grant and Papa were pretty exhausted," said Mimi. "You NEVER see Grant want to go to bed early."

"Besides that," said Christina, "he said he had a 'shrimp ache!'"

Everyone giggled.

"Well, I think I will join Papa and Grant!" said Mimi. "Close the screen to the fireplace before you go to sleep, Christina."

"I will," said Christina. "Good night, Mimi."

"Good night, girls," Mimi replied, giving them each a hug.

The rain pounded harder on the windowpanes and sky lights. The girls pulled their sleeping bags and pillows closer to the fire. After a few more s'mores, Avery opened her backpack and carefully removed the clues they had found.

"Look at all the clues we have, Christina," she said. She spread the pieces of paper out in front of her and read by the light of the fire.

"Clue One," read Avery in a serious tone. *"Barges sail far away. Enjoy Savannah the scouting way.* Clue Two. *Juliette, oh Juliette, where were thou born?"*

"That's my favorite clue," said Ella. She smiled, showing off the gap where her two front teeth used to be.

"Clue Three," continued Avery. *"Forsyth Park is where they like to play when lively scouts come this way."*

"Did you have fun at Forsyth Park?" asked Christina.

"We did!" said Amber. "We played 'Down by the Banks' with a lot of other Girl Scouts."

"We made new friends!" said Ella, hugging her knees.

Avery rolled her eyes. "Let's get back to the clues!" she said. "Clue Four. *Once a little girl named Daisy liked to roam the squares like crazy!* Clue Five. *Little Brownies come and go, but they always eat ice cream at Leopold's.*"

"Personally, I think that's the best clue so far!" said Grace. "Yuuuummy!"

"It WAS a pretty good clue," agreed Amber, shaking her head up and down.

Avery sighed. "Now, we have Clue Six," she said. *"Back when Girl Scouts were very new, they would meet in this house, too!"*

"Hmmm," said Christina. "Well, obviously, your ghost is talking about the Andrew Low Home. That's where Juliette Gordon Low lived when she started the Girl Scouts. I think some of the first troop meetings were held there."

"What do you think about our clues, Christina?" asked Avery.

"I hate to disappoint you, Avery," said Christina gently. "But like I said before, I think this is just some type of silly game. And you girls are going to the places so you are finding the clues."

"But what about the weird people who keep watching us?" asked Avery.

"Like who?" asked Christina.

"That weird, witchy tour guide," replied Avery. "And Igor the butler."

"Oh, please!" said Christina. "Don't pay any attention to them. They are always around Savannah. They're harmless."

Avery folded her arms, stuck out her lower lip, and gazed into the fire.

"Go to the Andrew Low House tomorrow!" said Christina. "See what happens."

"Can you come with us, Christina?" Ella pleaded.

"I will!" replied Christina. "Right now, though, I want to read a little about Mary Musgrove, the part-Indian woman who translated between the Native Americans and

General James Oglethorpe and his men. I'll be back in a little bit."

"Just like Sacagawea?" asked Avery.

Christina gave Avery a proud nod. "Sort of, yes. How would those men have accomplished all they did without those women?!"

"They wouldn't have!" yelled Avery.

"Girls rule!" yelled Ella.

"Girl Scouts rule!" cried Grace and Amber in unison.

After Christina left the room, the girls silently watched the fire burn. Black and red crackling embers created ghostly faces in the dying coals.

"I just remembered something!" exclaimed Amber. "I read about a new Girl Scout Badge. It's a Detective Badge just for Juniors!"

"I don't think we have a crime on our hands, Amber!" said Grace, plumping up her pillow.

"I'm just saying that maybe we can practice figuring out clues," replied Amber.

"You mean Daisies can't get a Detective Badge?" said Ella. Her eyes filled with tears. "I want a Detective Badge, too!"

"Oh, Ella, I'm sorry," said Amber. "It won't be long before you can get one. You'll be a Brownie, and then a Junior, before you know it!"

Avery picked up her clues, keeping them in order with the newest one on top.

CRACK!! A flash of lightning lit up the room, and a rumble of thunder roared.

Everyone jumped.

I don't think this is a scavenger hunt! Avery thought, grabbing her pillow. *And someone is definitely following us and leaving clues!*

BOOM!!! A low, deep rumble followed another flash of lightning.

And if it's not that creepy Igor or the witchy lady, she thought, *WHO is it? And what do they want us to find?*

CRACK!!! BOOM!!! Avery put her pillow over her head and shuddered. She felt pretty sure that whatever it was, they would NOT like it!

15

ROCKING CHAIRS AND GOOSEBUMPS!

The next morning the storm had passed, but the skies were still dark with gray clouds. Avery, Ella, Grace, Amber, and Christina walked up the steps of the Andrew Low House. A carved stone lion sat on a pedestal on each side of the wide stairway leading to the crimson front door.

Amber rubbed one of the lions' head. "I read that Juliette Gordon Low asked visitors to rub the lion's head," she said.

Ella backed up and rubbed the other lion's head.

Inside, the girls joined other scouts on a guided tour of the house that was the home of Juliette Gordon Low after she was married.

"This house was built in 1848 for Andrew Low, a wealthy businessman," said the guide. "His son, William Mackay Low, married Juliette Gordon in 1886. The couple lived and traveled in Europe for long periods. But they frequently stayed here from the time they were married until Mr. Low died in 1905."

"What happened after that?" asked Avery.

"The Lows were in the process of divorcing," said the tour guide. "But the paperwork was not complete when William Low died. So Juliette Gordon Low inherited the property."

"Look at this room," said Amber. "It says General Robert E. Lee slept here!"

"Yes," said the guide. "He visited Savannah after the Civil War in 1870 and was a guest here."

The tour guide told them how Juliette Gordon Low continued to travel after her husband died. She learned about the Girl Guides movement in England and Scotland.

"She came back to America in 1912," said the tour guide. "She was very excited and called her cousin. She said, 'Come right over! I've got something for the girls of Savannah, and all of America, and all the world, and we're going to start it tonight.'"

Avery, Ella, Christina, Amber, Grace, and all the other scouts on the tour beamed.

"Juliette Gordon Low and her cousin recruited girls from all over Savannah," said the tour guide. "On March 12, 1912, she founded the organization."

The girls stopped to look at a photo of Juliette Gordon Low and Girl Scouts holding the Founder's Banner in the courtyard of the Andrew Low House.

"Look at those uniforms," said Christina. "They are so cool!"

"Did the first scouts meet here?" asked Grace.

"I heard she possibly had some meetings here," said Amber. "She had meetings at her parents' home, too."

"That's the Birthplace, right?" said Ella. "Where we went yesterday?"

"That's right, Ella," said Christina.

The girls rushed to catch up with the guide again.

"Juliette Gordon Low let the Scouts use the Carriage House behind this house as their headquarters," said the guide. "In 1918, the

Andrew Low House became her Savannah residence. She died here in 1927."

"Does this house have any ghosts?" asked Avery.

"Of course!" said the guide. "Most every house in Savannah has ghosts! People have seen that rocking chair over there move with no one in it. And there have been sightings of an old woman lying on her deathbed."

Ella gasped.

"Don't worry, Ella," said Avery to her little sister. "Everything is OK. We're not going to see a rocking chair move or an old lady on her deathbed."

Even though Avery assured her little sister, she stared intently at the rocking chair as they passed by. And as she walked down the hallways of the Andrew Low House, she listened for giggling. She heard nothing, but soon felt an icy chill and looked down to see goosebumps as big as mosquito bites pop up on her arms.

16

A GHOST IN COATTAILS?

The girls walked through the garden of the Andrew Low House with the tour guide. The muggy air was filled with the fragrance of blooming flowers.

"This garden was planted in 1848," said the tour guide. "It is the only original Savannah garden that is open to the public. You can stroll through the garden at your leisure. Behind the garden is a building many of you may like to visit. It's the Carriage House!"

"What's a carriage house?" Ella whispered to Christina.

"It was a garage for horses and buggies!" Christina whispered back.

"Right after Juliette Gordon Low organized the Girl Scouts," said the tour guide, "she renovated the carriage house behind her home as a headquarters. It's now called First Headquarters. It is a Girl Scout museum and program center. There's also a gift shop."

After thanking the tour guide, the girls headed to the Carriage House.

"Wow!" said Amber, reading a historic marker in front of the Carriage House. "This building has been continuously used for Girl Scout activities longer than any other building in the country!"

"This is a cool place," Christina remarked. "I came here with my troop for a program."

Grace opened the door of the First Headquarters.

"I'm going to leave you for a little while," said Christina. "I need to work some more on my project. I might go to the Georgia Historical Society. I'll let you know."

The girls waved goodbye to Christina and walked inside First Headquarters. The building was crammed with jostling scouts. Laughter and chatter floated through the hallways. Girl Scouts were touring the museum. Several troops were taking programs, which were like short courses on a specific topic.

"This looks like fun!" said Grace.

"I really want to do this Early Years program," said Avery. She peeked into a doorway and watched scouts learn to make a bed—with a patient in it!

"They also learn signal flags," said Amber, looking at a brochure. "And Morse code, and how to tie a burglar with eight inches of rope!"

"Why do they learn that?" asked Ella in amazement.

"Be prepared!" said Grace, shrugging her shoulders.

The girls wandered through the museum in First Headquarters. They looked at all the old uniforms and books.

"My tummy is starting to grumble," said Grace. "I need a pick-me-up! In fact, I need one of those cupcakes again or maybe some ice cream!"

"Can we walk back through the garden first?" asked Ella. "I want to smell the daisies again!"

Avery took Ella's hand as they strolled through the garden, smelling daisies and taking pictures. It was starting to mist. The wind was blowing a little harder. Tall flowers and shrubs surrounding the garden paths swayed to and fro.

"Ahhh, girls!" said Amber. "Look, what I just found!" She held up a piece of paper with a shamrock on it. "It's a little smeared and hard to read."

Grace pulled a magnifying glass from her backpack. She held it over the note and read aloud:

> Haunted houses are all around, but Colonial Cemetery has ghosts to be found

The girls gasped!

Ella's hands flew to her wide-open mouth.

Avery spun around to look down the garden path. She was just in time to see the end of something black flip around a corner of the path.

Was it a skirt? Avery thought. *Or was it the coattails of an old butler's uniform?*

17

DUELING DEATHS AND YELLOW FEVER!

"It's only a couple of blocks," said Avery. Holding her iPod, she bolted out of the garden.

"Look, Avery!" said Grace, catching up with her. "I don't believe in ghosts, but I don't want to go poking around any cemeteries either!"

"We'll be OK," said Avery. "It's daylight. Ghosts don't come out in daylight—I don't think!"

The weather was getting mistier and drearier as the girls dashed up Abercorn Street to Colonial Park Cemetery.

"There it is!" said Avery, pointing to her right. "The main gate must be up ahead."

When they reached an arch with an eagle on top, Avery turned into the cemetery.

"I'm getting wet!" said Ella, stopping to open her backpack.

"I'm sorry, Ella," said Avery, helping her sister. She slipped on her own raincoat.

"There aren't many people here," said Grace.

"That's because the weather is getting worse," said Amber, pulling her hood over her head.

"No!" said Grace. "That's because people don't go walking through ancient cemeteries for no reason!"

The girls walked down paths through a forest of 200-year-old headstones. Long strands of Spanish moss hanging from live oaks swayed above their heads, sometimes tickling the backs of their necks and causing them to screech.

"Creepy!" said Grace, brushing a wisp of the moss out of her eyes.

"Ah, what are we looking for?" asked Ella.

Avery looked blank.

"Your sister doesn't want to tell you that we're looking for giggling ghosts," answered Grace.

Suddenly, the girls turned a corner and stopped in their tracks. Ahead, a lady in a long, black cape floated toward them. Her lantern glowed eerily in the mist.

"It's a dreary *daaaaaaay* to walk through a place of the dead," she said to the girls in a somber tone.

"It's that d-d-dreadful woman from Wright Square," stuttered Amber.

The woman floated to a stop in front of the girls, who stood huddled on the path. She held her lantern out in front of her and peered into their faces.

"This cemetery is *not* for the faint of heart," she warned, her voice deep and sinister. "Are *youuuuu* faint of heart?" she said, looking straight at Amber.

Amber gulped. She thought she might faint!

"This cemetery is more than 250 years old," the lady said. "There are many souls here. Many, many stories. More than 700 victims of the Yellow Fever Epidemic are buried in the back of this cemetery. Heaped together in a mass grave. That was in 1820.

They are *not happy*!" she moaned, shaking her head sadly. *"NOT HAAAAPPPYYY!"*

Grace's eyes grew wide. She wished the witchy lady would hush up before she woke the dead!

"This House of the Dead witnessed hundreds of dueling deaths," the lady said in a monotone voice. "That was back in the day when dueling solved a man's problems and saved his honor. Men dueled on these very grounds. And they died here, too."

Ella covered her ears with her hands.

"Then there were those heartless Yankees!" said the woman. Her somber tone became angry. "They plundered graves when they came to Savannah. They desecrated and looted them. Ten thousand people once were buried in this cemetery. But now, only 600 gravestones remain."

The woman swirled around and pointed toward a brick wall. "See that wall over there?" she asked. "Those are misplaced headstones. Imagine, a broken headstone with no body to mark! Those ruthless troops of General William Tecumseh Sherman marched from Atlanta to Savannah—this fair,

fair lady by the sea." Her voice grew higher. "And they took what they wanted!"

The lady in black lifted her lantern high. She swung around. Her damp, black skirts swirled. "Noooooooo, these souls are not happy!!" she moaned as she flounced past the girls and down the path.

The girls stood spellbound until the woman was out of sight, then bolted for the exit and ran smack dab into an old Confederate soldier. He tipped his Rebel cap and stared at them with piercing, light blue eyes, as if he could see through them. *But...could they see through him?*

The girls bumped past him—*and ran for their lives!*

18

THERE GOES THE GIGGLING GHOST!

The girls were two blocks from the cemetery before Amber slowed everyone down. "Where are we going?" she asked.

"Away from that cemetery!" cried Grace.

"I'm getting a text," said Avery, searching for the iPod in her rain jacket. "It's Christina. She's at the Georgia Historical Society. She wants us to meet her there. It's close to Forsyth Park."

"As long as she's not at a cemetery, I'm good," said Grace.

A few minutes later, the girls dashed past an iron picket fence and up the steep stone steps of the Georgia Historical Society. They pulled open a heavy, arched door and entered a massive library.

"This place looks like it's from an Indiana Jones movie!" exclaimed Amber.

Tall, arched windows looked down on rows of wooden bookcases. Glass globe lamps glowed over long, wooden worktables. Christina sat at a table, hunched over stacks of books.

"This place is scary," said Ella to Christina.

"No, a drizzly cemetery is scary!" said Grace, flopping down onto a bench beside Christina.

"Why were you guys at a cemetery when there are so many fun 'Girl Scout' things to do?" asked Christina, suspicious.

Avery rolled her blue eyes toward the library's mammoth ceiling.

"You guys aren't still chasing a giggling ghost, are you?" asked Christina.

"Actually, we think the giggling ghost is chasing us," explained Avery.

Christina laughed.

"Ella, I hope you've done a good turn daily and brought me a cupcake or something," said Christina to her little cousin.

"Oh, not yet, Christina," said Ella, sadly.

"Hey, that's OK!" said Christina. "I heard the weather is going to get worse. Why don't you guys stay here while I finish up?"

"Is there anything to eat?" asked Grace, searching her backpack. "I'm plumb out of cookies."

"No food around here that I know of," replied Christina. "But Mimi, Papa and Grant are going to pick us up, and we'll go somewhere and eat and have some fun! Just stop worrying about ghosts!"

"Maybe there's something in the basement," Grace said, still looking for something to eat. The girls followed her down a huge hallway, looking for the staircase to the basement. Avery walked with her head down, lost in thought.

"Avery, don't be sad about the mystery," said Amber. "Just because Christina solves mysteries, doesn't mean we have to."

"I'm not sad," said Avery. "I'm thinking. I saw someone in black leave the garden at the Andrew Low House right after we found that clue."

"Well," said Grace. "That explains it. The lady in black is the giggling ghost."

"Duh, Grace!" said Avery. "That lady couldn't giggle if you tickled her nose with Spanish moss!"

"OK, so I'm the silly one!" said Grace. "But the note told us to go to the cemetery. That woman was at the cemetery. And, I might add, she probably had a great time trying to scare us to death!"

"You mean," said Amber, "she had a great time scaring the stuffing out of us! And she didn't have to try very hard!"

The four girls started laughing hysterically.

Grace began to moan and wail. "*Looooook*, there's the staircase," she said dramatically, imitating the woman in black. She pretended to lift up a lantern. "*Followwwwww meeeeee* to the basement," she said, "where unhappy souls lurk among the boxes and books!"

Giggling and acting silly, the girls followed Grace down the steps.

"Wait a minute," said Grace in her normal voice. "What's this? Oh, man!"

She scooped up a piece of paper from the stairway landing. A faded shamrock was visible on the tattered sheet. She held it so the girls could see it, and Avery read it aloud:

Girl Scouts like to giggle, and I do, too!

Suddenly, they heard rustling and giggling above them in the hallway.

The girls looked at each other and sprinted up the stairs. From the top stair, they spied the back of Igor the butler and another figure ahead of him, stepping out into the drizzly weather.

Avery gasped. Her mind raced. "We have to follow him," she said. "I think I know who is leaving these notes!"

Amber grabbed Avery's arm. "Avery, Christina said to wait here. Mimi and Papa will be here soon! We can't go out in this rain!"

"You stay here, then," said Avery. "I have to find the Giggling Ghost."

Avery raced away. Amber, Grace, and Ella looked at each other.

"Ella, you need—" said Amber.

"No!" said Ella, chasing after Avery. "I'm going, too!"

Ella, Amber, and Grace caught up with Avery as she yanked open the heavy door to a thick fog and steady drizzle. Ahead of them in the distance and nearly lost in the foggy mist was Igor. He was holding up a big black umbrella and clumsily lurching down the street.

BOOM!! Angry clouds rumbled as the girls cautiously stepped into the pouring rain.

The wind whipped Avery's hair around her face. Wet strands stung her eyes. *I can't lose him*, she thought. Like lightning, a chill ran up her spine.

19

THUNDER MANSION!

The four girls pulled their raincoat hoods up over their heads. Then they grabbed hands. As carefully as possible, they ran down the rain-slick steps of the Georgia Historical Society.

BOOM!! Thunder rumbled. The rain pelted their bright yellow raincoats. They splashed through puddles as they rushed up the street. They dashed past a sign that said "Monterey Park." They slopped through the wet, green grass in the square. They passed an ornate white monument with a sign that said "Count Casimir Pulaski." Strands of Spanish moss whipped through the tendrils of their hair. Rain pelted their faces.

Avery kept her eyes on the large, black umbrella bobbing in the distance.

"It's so foggy, but I think that umbrella is covering Igor," yelled Avery to the girls. "He's going up those stairs!"

As the girls got closer, they could see that the stairs led to a rose-colored, stucco mansion near the square. The doors to the manse stood open, and the umbrella bounced inside. Then, the doors shut with a BLAM!

"Whew! Now, what?" asked Grace, slowing down to catch her breath. She whipped an umbrella out of her backpack and held it over the girls.

Just then, Amber's phone rang. "It's Christina," she said to the girls, reading her Caller ID in the rain. Amber grimaced as she answered her cell phone. "Oh, hi, Christina!" she said merrily. "You did? Hold on." Amber looked at Avery. "Christina saw us leave, and she is following us. She wants to know where we are."

"Here, give her our coordinates," said Avery, handing her iPod to Amber.

"Christina says to tell you she is with your Mimi and Papa," said Amber. "They will be here to get us in a minute."

Just then, the door of the mansion swung open, and Igor stood in the doorway.

"Would you girls like to come out of the storm?" he yelled.

"Only if we can see the giggling ghost!" Avery yelled back fearlessly.

Igor waved them toward him and opened the mansion door wide.

BOOM!! BOOM!!! The thunder roared. Rain poured down on the girls.

Avery bolted toward the steps of the mansion with Grace close behind. Amber grabbed Ella's hand and followed them up the long, tall, marble staircase with iron railings and into the darkness of the manse.

BOOM!!

Struck by lightning or trapped in an old mansion with a ghost—some choice! thought Avery.

20

WHAT HAVE WE DONE?!

Avery blinked, trying to adjust her eyes to the dimness of the foyer.

CRACK!! Lightning pierced the windows of the old manse.

Rainwater ran down Avery's slick raincoat and dripped onto the marble tile floor with a splat, splat, splat. She gazed at an ornate staircase that spiraled up three floors from the foyer. She listened to the rain pelting the domed ceiling above them. *SPLAT! SPLAT! SPLAT!* It was like they were under attack.

BOOM!! Thunder shook the house to its crumbling core.

Igor's dripping wet, black umbrella stood propped against an umbrella stand. A long, gray, wet raincoat hung from a brass coat rack.

Igor closed the heavy wooden door and shuffled toward them. He was even skinnier up close. His thin, white hair clung in wet strands to the sides of his head. He kept his eyes lowered. He nervously rubbed his fingers together.

He handed each of the girls a fluffy, pale yellow towel from a pile stacked on an antique side table.

"Are you the giggling ghost?" asked Ella shyly.

"He's not the giggling ghost!" Avery assured her sister. "*But* he has been following her! And the giggling ghost is here in this house, isn't she?"

Just then, a crackly old voice called from the next room, "Timothy, please bring them to see me. I have been so hoping they would come!"

Timothy bowed low and said, "Follow me."

It was clearly an order.

He led the four girls into a bright yellow room. Pale yellow velvet drapes hung from the ceiling to the floor. Yellow fabric with blue flowers covered the chairs. Brass lamps filled the room with light.

An old woman with long gray hair pulled back with a gray satin ribbon sat on a blue and white sofa. A large bouquet of bright yellow daisies lay on her lap. She peered at the girls with cataract-covered, crinkly old eyes.

Avery stole a glance at the other girls. They looked petrified.

What have I done, she thought, *marching right into this strange, eerie house where we know no one and probably have no business being?*

The consequences of what she had done raced through Avery's mind. She started to grab the girls and run. *But would Igor stop us if we ran,* she wondered. *Was this woman a ghastly ghost or just a strange old woman?*

Just when Avery could stand the suspense no longer, the old woman steered her face toward the girls and reached out her gnarled, arthritic hands.

And then, she...giggled!

21

A DAISY FOR YOUR GIGGLE!

"Here is our giggling ghost!" Avery said to the girls. "I caught a glimpse of your daisies when you left the Georgia Historical Society," she said, turning toward the old lady. "I remembered the basket of daisies from our first day in Savannah. You were walking on the riverfront."

"May I introduce Miss Agnes Cornett," said Timothy, with an Irish lilt to his voice. "She is a direct descendant of some of the first settlers of Savannah."

He bowed and motioned the girls to come closer to the old lady.

"Call me Miss Aggie," the old lady said kindly. "Yes, yes, I did see you on the waterfront. I saw you do that lovely ceremony with your little boats. It made me miss Girl Scouts so much. I was born the same year dear Juliette Gordon Low organized the Girl Scouts."

"Are you 100 years old?" asked Grace. "I've never known someone who is 100 years old!"

"I am, dear!" said Miss Aggie. "I was a Girl Scout when I was a girl. We used to meet in the Carriage House behind Miss Juliette's house. She was so busy starting the Scouts. But she came to our meetings sometimes. I loved those days! I loved being a Girl Scout!"

"But why have you and Igor—uh, I mean Mr. Timothy—been following us?" asked Avery. "I couldn't figure that out. And why have you been sending us these clues?"

"Oh, dear, Timothy!" she said to her butler. "I didn't want to frighten them. Do you think we frightened them? Did I frighten you, dear?" she said, turning to Avery. She wrung her hands and looked nervous.

"I never thought the giggling ghost would hurt us," said Avery. "I just wanted to figure out who you were."

Miss Agnes brightened. "I wanted to make sure you did all the things Girl Scouts do when they come to Savannah. I wanted to watch you do them. I just wanted to be a Girl Scout one more time!"

Avery moved toward Miss Agnes. She held out her left hand to Miss Agnes and made the Girl Scout sign with her right. Miss Agnes took Avery's hand and made the Girl Scout sign with her right hand. They shook hands.

One by one, Ella, Grace, and Amber came forward and did the scout handshake with Miss Agnes.

Tears of joy filled Miss Agnes' old eyes as she handed each girl a handful of yellow daisies.

BANG! BANG! BANG! A heavy doorknocker hit the front door.

Timothy rushed out of the room.

"I guess we know who that is," said Avery, shaking her head. All the girls were nervous. The only thing scarier than a ghost was Mimi when she was upset!

They heard voices in the foyer, and then Mimi burst into the room with Papa, Christina, and Grant close behind.

"Avery!" cried Mimi. "You have worried us to death! Why did you leave Christina, and what is going on here?"

"I'm sorry, Mimi," said Avery. "Something got into me. I had to solve the mystery of the giggling ghost!"

Ella turned to Mimi with daisies in her hands and said softly, "We did a good turn today, Mimi!"

22

A CIRCLE OF FRIENDSHIP!

Timothy served tea and Girl Scout cookies as Miss Agnes told stories about her days as a Girl Scout.

"Here are some more cookies for you, Miss Ella," he said, his blue eyes twinkling.

"Thank you, Mr. Timothy," said Ella, taking lemony cookies from a plate.

"Did you learn Morse code when you were a Girl Scout?" asked Avery.

"We certainly did," said Miss Agnes. She tapped her fingers on a table and giggled. "We marched everywhere. We learned signal flags and how to make bandages. We hiked through the woods in our knee-length uniforms. We played basketball and went on camping trips. Of course, it was unheard of for girls to do those types of things back then! That's one reason why Girl Scouts was so much fun!"

"Lets make a Friendship Circle," said Christina.

Each of them crossed their right arm over the left arm of the person standing next to them. Then, they clasped hands. Starting with Christina, everyone made a silent wish as they passed a friendship squeeze from hand to hand.

"Why don't you girls visit Miss Agnes again after the Camporee?" said Mimi as they were leaving.

Miss Agnes giggled. "That would be wonderful!" she said.

"We'll bring you pictures!" said Grace.

"We'll tell you about everything we did!" said Avery.

"I'll make sure you get lots of things to read about the Camporee!" added Amber.

Timothy scurried to the front door and opened it wide. Sunshine streamed into the foyer. The storm was over and so was the mystery. They stepped out onto the steps. The sky was blue, and loads of scouts were roaming around the streets of Savannah again.

They walked away, waving to Timothy and Miss Agnes, who blew kisses to everyone.

Grant shoved a mint cookie into his mouth. "I'm sure glad Miss Agnes had some of these," he said. "I'm pretty sure we're out!"

"I KNOW we're out!" replied Grace. "Thanks to you!"

Everyone laughed.

Avery, Ella, Amber, Grace, and Christina stuck Miss Agnes' daisies into their hair. Then, they put their arms around each other and skipped away—happy to be friends—happy to be Girl Scouts!

But most especially, happy to be mystery-solving scouts. *Maybe a Junior Detective Badge was possible after all*, thought Avery, and she giggled.

131

About the Author

Carole Marsh is the Founder and CEO of Gallopade International, an award-winning, woman-owned family business founded in 1979 that publishes books and other materials intended to guide, inspire and inform children of all ages. Marsh is best known for her children's mystery series called **Real Kids! Real Places! America's National Mystery Book Series.** Popular among children ages 7-14, this series follows four characters (Mimi, Papa, Christina, and Grant) along educational adventures to more than 48 locations across the U.S. *Learning* Magazine has awarded the series with the Teacher's Choice Award for the Family, and Midwest Book Review called her mysteries for children "true gems of education and entertainment for young readers."

During her 30 years as a children's author, Marsh has been honored with several recognitions including Georgia Author of the

Year and Communicator of the Year. She has also received the iParenting Award for Greatest Products, the Excellence in Education award, and been honored for Best Family Books by *Learning* Magazine. She is also the author of *Mary America, First Girl President of the United States*, winner of the 2012 Teacher's Choice Award for the Family from *Learning* Magazine.

Over the years, Marsh has been the creative force for more than 15,000 supplemental educational materials that Gallopade currently publishes. Other popular series include all nine Carole Marsh Mystery series, The Student's Civil War graphic novels for kids, the State Stuff series which is available for all 50 states, American Milestones reproducible resource books, and many more!

For more information about Carole Marsh and Gallopade International, please visit www.gallopade.com.

GIRL SCOUT GLOSSARY

BADGE
Round embroidered award for Junior and Cadette Girl Scouts to indicate increased knowledge and skill in a particular subject.

BRIDGING
Activities designed to emphasize the continuity of the Girl Scout program, to introduce girls within each age level to what lies ahead, and to give older girls a sense of personal responsibility for younger girls.

BUDDY SYSTEM
A safety practice in which girls of equal ability are paired to help and to keep track of each other.

CLOSING
Any standard activity that signals the end of a meeting (i.e., Friendship Circle, song, etc.).

COURT OF AWARDS
A ceremony that can be held any time during the year at which badges and other awards are presented.

DUNK BAG
A netted bag used to hang washed dishes to dry in the outdoors.

FLAG CEREMONY
A Girl Scout ceremony involving not only the U.S. flag, but flags of the troop, the Council or of Girl Guide nations.

FLY UP
The ceremony in which a Brownie Girl Scout "graduates" to Junior Girl Scouts. We also call this ceremony "Bridging."

FRIENDSHIP CIRCLE
A symbolic gesture in which girls form a circle by clasping each others' hands, often used as a closing ceremony.

FRIENDSHIP SQUEEZE
A hand squeeze passed around a Friendship Circle.

GIRL AWARD SILVER AWARD
The highest award in Girl Scouting earned by a Cadette Girl Scout.

GIRL GUIDE
The original name for Girl Scouts, still used in many countries.

GIRL SCOUT SIGN
The official Girl Scout greeting. It is always used when the Promise is made or repeated. The right hand is raised shoulder high, palm forward, with the three middle fingers extended and the thumb holding down the little finger.

INVESTITURE
A special ceremony in which a new member makes her Girl Scout Promise and receives her membership pin.

JULIETTES
(Part of the Girl Scout My Way Pathway for girls.) Individual members not affiliated with a troop. All rights and principals are extended to Juliettes.

KAPER CHART
A chart that shows the delegation of jobs and rotation of responsibility day by day and/or meal by meal.

LEADER
An adult member of the organization who meets with a troop/group of girls to help it achieve the purpose of Girl Scouting, and has completed the required leadership training.

MOTTO
"Be Prepared." A motto adopted as a guiding principle for members.

PATCHES AND PINS
Supplementary insignia whose focus is participation, not prescribed requirements. These awards are sewn onto the back of a girls' vest or sash.

QUIET SIGN
A traditional technique for obtaining silence at all Girl Scout meetings, made by raising the right hand. Group members raise their hands and become quiet until complete silence is established.

SASH/VEST
A part of the Girl Scout uniform where the girl may display her Girl Scout recognitions and insignia.

SIT-UPONS
Something to sit on.

S'MORES
A favorite campfire treat consisting of graham crackers, chocolate bars and toasted marshmallows.

SWAPS
"Special Whachamacalits Affectionately Pinned Somewhere." Small items used for trading at events.

TREFOIL
The official emblem of the Girl Scout movement in the United States of America, registered in the United States Patent Office by Girl Scouts of the U.S.A.

WORLD ASSOCIATION OF GIRL GUIDES AND GIRL SCOUTS (WAGGGS)
The international organization of Girl Guide/Girl Scout associations organized in 1928.

WORLD THINKING DAY
February 22, the birthday of both Lord and Lady Baden-Powell, celebrated as the day in which Girl Guides and Girl Scouts all over the world think of each other and exchange greetings.

TALK ABOUT IT!

*Book Club Discussion Questions
for a Class or Troop*

1. Savannah is a beautiful, historic city. Name one thing you learned about Savannah's history by reading this book. Do you like to visit places and learn about their history?

2. The characters in the mystery enjoy one of Savannah's specialties—wild Georgia shrimp. Name one reason why different locations have their own special types of food. Are you willing to try new things when you visit new places? If so, can you think of something you really liked? What about something you did not like?

3. The Girl Scouts planned a Camporee to celebrate the 100th anniversary of the founding of their organization. 100 years is a long time! Why do you think people celebrate anniversaries?

4. The girls visited many of Savannah's historic locations in the book. What was your favorite place? Why? What place were you able to picture most vividly in your mind?

5. Avery's GPS locator came in quite handy. Do you know what "GPS" stands for? What does a GPS help you do? Have you ever used one?

6. What was the scariest part of the mystery? What was the funniest?

7. Which character did you like the most? Which character was most like you?

8. Juliette Gordon Low dealt with a handicap during her life. What was her handicap? How would you feel if you lost that sense?

9. Throughout the mystery, one character attempts to do a good turn daily. Which character did that? Do you try to do something to help another person each day?

BRING IT TO LIFE!

*Book Club Activities
for a Class or Scout Troop*

1. Pick a famous historical figure from Savannah. Use books or the Internet to learn interesting things about that person's life. Dress up and "impersonate" your choice at your book club meeting.

2. Create a new "square" for Savannah! Make it a square honoring the Girl Scouts. Draw your square on a poster board. Add pictures or drawings of the things you would display in your square to honor the Girl Scouts!

3. Set up an acrostic poem using the word "Savannah." Challenge your book club members to use every letter in the word to write something special about the city!

4. Write the names of every character in the mystery on separate slips of paper. Fold the slips and put them in a box. Ask each book club member to select a slip of paper from the box, and pretend they are that character. Go around the room, giving everyone a chance to ask each character questions to figure out who they are. Ideas for questions are: "Are you a male or a female?" "What makes you so important to the story?" "When do you first appear in the story?"

5. Map it out! On a large map of the United States, map out the route you would take from your home state to Savannah, Georgia. List the states you would pass through. Would you rather fly there on an airplane or drive there? Would you have to cross any major mountain range? Would you have to cross the Mississippi River? Which direction would you head—north, south, east, or west?

SCAVENGER HUNT

Let's go on a Savannah Scavenger Hunt! See if you can find the items below related to the mystery and the city of Savannah, and then write the page number where you found each one. (*Teachers: You have permission to reproduce this page for your students.*)

_____ 1. Savannah Dan

_____ 2. Live oak trees

_____ 3. Boulder marking Tomochichi's grave

_____ 4. Juliette Gordon Low Birthplace

_____ 5. Forsyth Fountain

_____ 6. Statue of James Oglethorpe

_____ 7. Leopold's Ice Cream

_____ 8. Some s'mores

_____ 9. A house with a room where Robert E. Lee slept

_____10. A cemetery where graves were plundered by Union soldiers

GIRL SCOUTS BY GRADE LEVEL

Daisy – grades K-1

Brownie – grades 2-3

Junior – grades 4-5

Cadette – grades 6-8

Senior – grades 9-10

Ambassador – grades 11-12

FAMOUS GIRL SCOUTS

Did you know that many of today's female American leaders were once Girl Scouts? Here's a list of some famous Girl Scouts:

🍀 **Laura Bush** (First Lady of the United States)

🍀 **Hillary Rodham Clinton** (Secretary of State for President Obama; U.S. Senator; First Lady of the United States)

🍀 **Nancy Reagan** (First Lady of the United States)

🍀 **Chelsea Clinton** (daughter of President Bill Clinton)

🍀 **Condoleezza Rice** (Secretary of State for President George W. Bush)

🍀 **Lt. Col. Eileen Collins** (astronaut; first woman Space Shuttle Commander)

🍀 **Sally Ride** (astronaut; first American woman in space)

🍀 **Mae Jemison** (first African American woman in space)

Sandra Day O'Connor (Associate Justice of the U.S. Supreme Court)

Katie Couric (TV journalist)

Danica Patrick (race car driver)

Dorothy Hamill (Olympic figure skating champion)

Jackie Joyner-Kersee (Olympic track and field champion)

Venus Williams (professional tennis player)

Taylor Swift (singer and entertainer)

Mariah Carey (singer and entertainer)

Abigail Breslin (actress)

Dakota Fanning (actress)

Carole Gist (first African American Miss USA)

Vera Wang (fashion designer)

Pam Fields (founder of Mrs. Fields Cookies)

MIMI'S FAVORITE SAVANNAH PLACES TO VISIT!

- Savannah Dan's charming tours! Go to www.savannahdan.com

- Magnolia Gifts at 137 Bull Street on Wright Square is Halloween Central with their year-round Halloween Room!

- Just 4 Kids has a great toy store both on River Street and out at cool Sandfly!

- At The Paris Market on Broughton Street, you'll feel like you've entered a movie set. Be sure to go to the basement!

- Don't miss Leopold's Ice Cream on Broughton for truly homemade ice cream and special flavors for special events, like Thin Mints and Cream and Savannah Smiles for the Girl Scouts!

- Mabel Francis Potter's Cupcake Emporium near the corner of Bull and State Streets will satisfy your sweet tooth!

OTHER GALLOPADE BOOKS SET IN GEORGIA

The Awesome Atlanta Mystery

The Ghosts of Pickpocket Plantation

The Mystery at Fort Thunderbolt

The Secret of Skullcracker Swamp

The Secret of Eyesocket Island

That's Soooo Savannah Coloring Book

The Student's Civil War Georgia Reproducible Activity Book

OTHER BOOKS TO READ

Juliette Gordon Low: Founder of the Girl Scouts by Carole Marsh

Here Come the Girl Scouts! The Amazing All-True Story of Juliette "Daisy" Gordon Low and Her Great Adventure by Shana Corey

Juliette Gordon Low: The Remarkable Founder of the Girl Scouts by Stacy A. Cordery

First Girl Scout: The Life of Juliette Gordon Low by Ginger Wadsworth

On My Honor: Real Life Lessons from America's First Girl Scout by Shannon Kleiber

Lady from Savannah: The Life of Juliette Low by Daisy Gordon Lawrence

Girl Scouts: A Celebration of 100 Trailblazing Years by Betty Christiansen

Enjoy this exciting excerpt from:

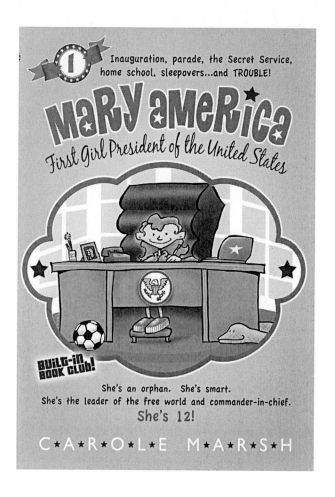

Prologue

IT WAS STRANGE how it happened. Millard Standish Willoughby was elected president of the United States. His wife had died ten years earlier of cancer. Their oldest daughter, Abigail, had been a lawyer. She had married another lawyer, Joseph America. While on assignment in a war zone for the U.S. military, they had both been killed in a bomb attack on a courthouse.

And so when President Willoughby took office and came to live in the White House, he brought his two orphaned grandchildren, Mary and Josh, with him.

President Willoughby adored them both, but was especially fond of the oldest, Mary.

She had her mother's beautiful skin, eyes, and hair, and she was smart. She had already skipped several grades in school, and was eligible to go on to college. Instead, Mary held the Bible while her grandfather took the oath of office, marched down Pennsylvania Avenue on a blue-sky, winter's day in the Inauguration parade, and settled into the White House at her grandfather's side.

During his first two years of office, President Willoughby had been exceedingly effective. He was decisive, popular, a good man at getting people on opposite sides of the fence to listen, learn, and, even if gritting their teeth, agree. It was hard to pinpoint exactly when his health began to fail. Like former president Franklin D. Roosevelt, who suffered from polio, the folks who surrounded him helped cover up President Willoughby's almost imperceptible, but growing, disabilities.

At first it was just a little forgetfulness. But slowly things grew worse. An energetic man, he began to need frequent "catnaps" to get through the day. Almost no one outside of his immediate circle of aides, closest friends, the White House physician, and his granddaughter, of course, realized that the robust man had changed.

On the surface, the White House and the world went on, President Willoughby always there to give press conferences, meet with heads of state, kick-off the annual Easter Egg Roll, and other presidential duties, slight and serious.

As always, Mary, nicknamed by the media the "Little First Lady" (a term she did not care for), was nearby. She spent time in the Oval Office, attended many meetings, and "to witness history," as her grandfather put it, could even be found in the tense Situation Room of the White House during a crisis.

On November 21, precisely at midnight, President Millard Standish Willoughby had a heart attack and died. In the hours that followed, it was discovered that after a former law had been changed to allow a certain California governor to run for president (in spite of not being a native-born American), a minor, but dramatic, alteration had subsequently been made and signed into law by President Willoughby. This clause changed the requirements related to the age limits for presidential eligibility. Indeed, any age limits at all had been removed.

The new stipulation specified no age, but that the candidate must have an IQ of at least 140. Another law had been added specifying that if a president could not finish his term, he could name a successor to finish that term. At 11:59 p.m. on the night of November 21, President Willoughby, White House lawyer at his side, had inked in his choice. The document had been notarized.

At 1:17 a.m. on November 22, Mary America, IQ 146, had been sworn in as the new President of the United States. The Bible she swore the oath on had rested on her deceased grandfather's chest. As required, Mary completed the oath by saying in a quiet, but assured voice: "I do solemnly swear." She then bent over and kissed her beloved grandfather goodbye on his forehead. She thus became the new commander-in-chief and leader of the free world.

President Mary America was twelve years old.

Five months later...
Monday, 9:00 a.m.
The Oval Office

BECAUSE HER FEET would not reach the floor, a small footstool had been placed beneath the presidential desk in the Oval Office for Mary America to rest her feet on. Whenever she sat at her desk (one that had once belonged to President Franklin D. Roosevelt), she always peeked beneath first to see if either "Ssss," her big, green boa constrictor, or Josh, her pesky younger brother, were hiding there.

The reason she had to check was that Josh would often sneak down there while Mary was doing some presidential concentrating and tie her shoe- laces together so that when she tried to stand up, she tripped. And Ssss had learned how to untie her shoelaces, so when she tried to stand up, she also got entangled and tripped.

Mary did not like to trip up. She took being President very seriously. It was a hard job. Being smart made it easier. Being a kid made it harder. People often thought they could "trip Mary up" because she was just twelve years old, but they soon learned better.

Nonetheless, it did not help a President to fall flat on her face when greeting the Secretary of State or the Queen of England. So Mary always checked her shoes—twice.

This morning, Josh was at school. He was lucky that he got to go to public school, Mary thought. Her other grandfather (referred to as the First Gramps by the media), who lived with them in the White House, had insisted that Josh not be escorted by the Secret Service to school.